This book belongs to:

_____

Other books in the series:

Magic Wand

Best Friends

Magic Sprinkles

Copyright © 2011 make believe ideas ltd.
The Wilderness, Berkhamsted, Hertfordshire, HP4 2AZ, UK.
565 Royal Parkway, Nashville, TN 37214, USA.

Reading together

This book is designed to be fun for children who are just starting to read on their own. They will enjoy and benefit from some time discussing the story with an adult. Encourage them to pause and talk about what is happening in the pictures. Help them to spot familiar words and sound out the letters in harder words. Look at the following ways you can help your child take those first steps in reading:

Look at rhymes

The sentences in this book are written with simple rhymes. Encourage your child to recognize the rhyming words. Try asking the following questions:

• What does this word say?

• Can you find a word that rhymes with it?

• Look at the ending of two rhyming words – are they spelled the same? For example, "neat" and "treat."

Test understanding

It is one thing to understand one word at a time, but it is important to make sure your child can understand the story as a whole!

Ask your child questions as you read the story, for example:

• What food and drink does Camilla make for the party?

• When does the party start?

• How does Camilla get her new cupcakes and tea?

• Play "find the obvious mistake." Read the text as your child looks at the words with you, but make an obvious mistake to see if he or she catches it. Ask your child to correct you and provide the right word.

Activity section

A "Ready to tell" section at the end of the book encourages children to remember what happened in the story and then retell it. A dictionary page helps children to increase their vocabulary, and a useful word page reinforces their knowledge of the most common words. There is also a practical activity inspired by the story and a "Camilla and her friends" section where children can learn about all of Camilla the Cupcake Fairy's friends!

Every day
at a quarter to three,
Camilla has a party,
with pink fairy tea!

Camilla makes cupcakes
and piles them high –
pink cupcake mountains
that reach for the sky!

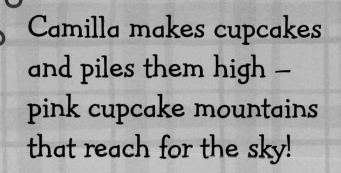

And with a wave of her wand,
as a finishing touch,
she makes frosting and sprinkles,
but never too much!

Sweet strawberry tea,
always served hot,
is poured from the
pinkest fairy teapot.

Camilla takes sugar and sometimes whipped cream. Her swirls are the twirliest and highest you've seen!

When the table is set,
and her house is neat,
Camilla is ready for her
favorite pink treat!

But one day Camilla
was feeling so sad –
her cakes did not rise
and the tea tasted bad!

The table she laid
was a real disgrace,
with spoons, plates, and napkins
all over the place!

She looked at her clock —
nearly half past two!
It was all such a mess,
but what could she do?

Then just when she needed
good luck the most,
Sandy arrived with
the pink fairy post.

She had a pink package
with all you could need
for a pink fairy party
to surely succeed.

Camilla opened the package,
as quickly as could be.
She found some pink cupcakes
and sweet strawberry tea!

The party was perfect
and no one could guess
that moments before
there had been such a mess!

Ready to tell

Can you remember what happened in the story? Look at each picture and then try retelling the story.

5

6

7

8

23

Camilla's fairy dictionary

mess If something is in a mess, it is not very tidy or is all mixed up.

package A package is something that you send in the mail. It is usually packed in a box or wrapped up in paper.

quickly If you do something quickly, you do it very fast or in a very short amount of time.

reach When you reach for something, you stretch out to move towards it or take hold of it.

sprinkles Sprinkles are tiny pieces of sugar that are often brightly colored. They are used to decorate cupcakes or desserts.

Camilla's useful words

Here are some key words used in context. Make simple sentences for the other words in the border.

Camilla has parties **with** pink fairy tea.

She makes cupcakes with frosting **on** top.

One day, the cupcakes **would** not rise.

A package **came** to save the day.

Camilla **put** the cupcakes and tea on the table.

Camilla and her friends

Camilla loves making cupcakes and using her wand to make magical toppings! She sometimes gets a little confused, but she never gives up and is a true friend to the other cupcake fairies.

Connie loves art and crafts. She's always drawing, painting, or gluing. Most of all, she loves making gifts for her friends.

Molly is kind, thoughtful, and a bit of a dreamer. She's always coming up with new things to do and try. Sometimes they are a little crazy!

Maya is super-smart. She's always reading recipe books and inventing new cakes and toppings. Her favorite day of the year is Cupcake Day when all the fairies have a bake-off!

Carrie is full of energy, and she is always on the go! She loves rushing around on her roller skates and is crazy about all sports, especially soccer.

Sally Swish runs the Wanderful wand shop. She sells every kind of wand you can imagine!

Cranberry is Camilla's cat. He's a little lazy but loves to join in Camilla's adventures – especially if they involve cupcakes, which they usually do!

Miss Sprinkles

is the cupcake fairies' teacher. She is very kind and wise and will always help the fairies if they have a problem.

Sandy Swirls has a very

important job: delivering the fairy mail! On a cupcake fairy's fifth birthday, Sandy delivers their very first magic wand.

Camilla's cupcake recipe!

Ingredients (makes 12):

2 large eggs
$^1/_2$ cup / 125 g sugar
$^1/_2$ cup / 125 g soft margarine
$^1/_2$ cup / 125 g self-rising flour

Always ask
an adult to
help you!

Optional toppings:

powdered sugar / food coloring,
marshmallows, chocolate drops,
sprinkles, colored candies